Mr. P(Hedge

written by Elizabeth Pulford   illustrated by Karactaz

KAEDEN ♥ BOOKS™

Mr. Potter went outside and looked at his hedge. It had grown too tall. It needed to be cut.

Mr. Potter went into his shed. He found his ladder. He found his chain saw. One by one he took them outside.

He climbed up the ladder. He started up the chain saw, and cut along the top of the hedge.

"It's crooked," called out his neighbor.

Mr. Potter cut some more.

"It's still crooked," yelled out the other neighbor.

Mr. Potter turned off the chain saw. He
climbed down from the ladder and took
a look.

The top of the hedge looked like a wiggling worm.

"Oh, dear," said Mr. Potter.

This time when he went into his shed, he picked up a pair of hand clippers. He picked up an old wooden chair too. Then Mr. Potter went back to the hedge.

He climbed onto the wooden chair.
He clipped along the top of the hedge.

"It's full of spikes," called out his neighbor.

Mr. Potter cut some more. Faster and faster went the hand clippers.

"It's still full of spikes," yelled out his other neighbor.

Mr. Potter jumped off the chair and took a look. The top of the hedge looked like a spiky hedgehog.

"Oh, dear," said Mr. Potter.

Mr. Potter went back into his shed. He found a pair of garden scissors and a wooden step. Then he went back to the hedge.

He climbed onto the step and started
to work.

"It's a mess," called out his neighbor.

"It's a big mess," yelled out his other neighbor.

Mr. Potter took no notice.

When he had finished he hopped off the step and looked at the hedge. He smiled. It was perfect.